IN THE NIGHT KITCHEN

MAURICE SENDAK

HARPER & ROW, PUBLISHERS

ISBN 0-06-443086-3

FOR SADIE AND PHILIP

DID YOU EVER HEAR OF MICKEY, HOW HE HEARD A RACKET IN THE NIGHT

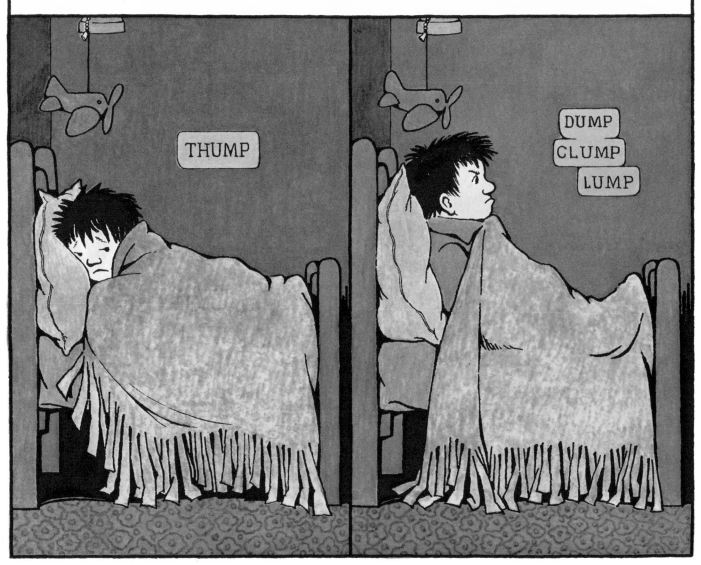

AND SHOUTED

QUIET DOWN THERE!

AND FELL THROUGH THE DARK, OUT OF HIS CLOTHES

PAST THE MOON & HIS MAMA & PAPA SLEEPING TIGHT

AND THEY PUT THAT BATTER UP TO BAKE

A DELICIOUS MICKEY-CAKE.

SO HE SKIPPED FROM THE OVEN & INTO BREAD DOUGH ALL READY TO RISE IN THE NIGHT KITCHEN.

TILL IT LOOKED OKAY.

WHEN THE BAKERS RAN UP
WITH A MEASURING CUP, HOWLING:

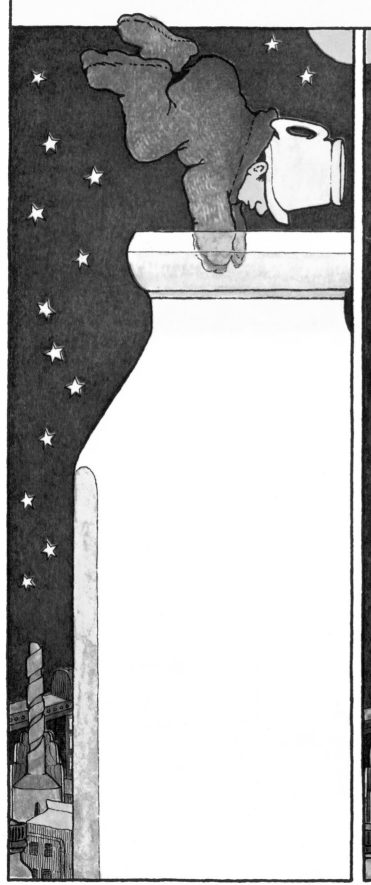

SO THE BAKERS THEY MIXED IT AND BEAT IT AND BAKED IT.